Disney's HERCULES

Adapted by Margaret Snyder
Illustrated by Cardona Studio

WALT DISNEY PICTURES PRESENTS **"HERCULES"**
MUSIC BY ALAN MENKEN   LYRICS BY DAVID ZIPPEL   ORIGINAL SCORE BY ALAN MENKEN
SCREENPLAY BY RON CLEMENTS & JOHN MUSKER, BOB SHAW & DON McENERY AND IRENE MECCHI
PRODUCED BY ALICE DEWEY AND JOHN MUSKER & RON CLEMENTS
DIRECTED BY JOHN MUSKER & RON CLEMENTS
DISTRIBUTED BY BUENA VISTA PICTURES DISTRIBUTION © DISNEY ENTERPRISES, INC.

🅖 A GOLDEN BOOK • NEW YORK

Golden Books Publishing Company, Inc., Racine, Wisconsin 53404

Long ago, in ancient Greece, there lived a young man named Hercules. From the time Hercules was a baby, everyone was amazed by his incredible strength. But being so strong was a problem—Hercules seemed to break everything he touched. Shunned because of the destruction he caused, Hercules grew up sad and lonely.

"I'll never fit in around here," Hercules told Amphitryon and Alcmene, the kind couple who had found him as an infant and raised him as their own.

Finally Amphitryon explained to Hercules that he was indeed different from everyone else.

"This was around your neck when we found you," the kind man said, handing Hercules a shiny medallion. "It's the symbol of the gods."

Eager to solve the mystery of his birth, Hercules traveled to the Temple of Zeus, king of the gods, for answers. He was shocked when the statue of Zeus came alive and the god revealed that *he* was Hercules' father— and that the goddess Hera was his mother.

Zeus explained that Hercules had been kidnapped and changed into a mortal while still a baby. Then he told Hercules why he could not come home.

"Only gods can live on Mount Olympus," he said. "But if you can prove yourself a true hero on Earth, your godhood will be restored.

"First," he continued, "you must seek out Philoctetes, the trainer of heroes."

Zeus gave Hercules the gift of a winged horse named Pegasus. Hercules flew off and soon found Philoctetes, the satyr. "I need your help," Hercules told Phil. "I want to become a hero, a true hero."

"Sorry, kid," said Phil. "I'm retired." But a lightning bolt from Zeus changed Phil's mind.

Hero-training was so difficult that Hercules often thought of quitting. In the end, though, he refused to give up and kept on working to reach his goal.

Finally Phil told Hercules that he was ready for his first real test—in the big, tough city of Thebes.

"If you can make it in Thebes, you can make it anywhere," said Phil.

On their way to Thebes, Phil and Hercules saw
a beautiful young woman named Megara, who
was being chased by a centaur.
"A damsel in distress!" Phil shouted. Hercules
rushed to Megara's rescue.

After Hercules had defeated the centaur, Megara introduced herself. "My friends call me Meg," she said. "What's your name?"

Hercules was so enchanted by Meg's beauty, he could barely speak. "I'm . . . uh . . . Hercules," he stammered.

"I prefer Wonder Boy," said Meg.

On her way home, Meg met Hades, the god of the Underworld, and his helpers, Pain and Panic. Meg mentioned that she had just met someone named Hercules.

Hercules! Hades was furious when he heard the name. He had ordered Pain and Panic to get rid of Hercules years before. Hercules was the only one who could stop the evil Hades from taking over Olympus.

Hades began trying to destroy Hercules once again. He used Meg to trick Hercules into unleashing a frightening monster called the Hydra. But Hercules defeated the Hydra and every other monster that Hades sent. And with each victory, Hercules became more and more famous.

Still Hercules remained a mortal—unable to live on Olympus. Hercules asked Zeus why this was so.

"I'm afraid being famous isn't the same as being a true hero," Zeus answered. "You must look inside your heart."

Hades finally realized that no one was strong enough to defeat Hercules. Still, Hades thought, he must have *one* weakness. . . .

Suddenly Hades knew the answer: Meg was Hercules' one weakness. Hercules would do *anything* to protect her from harm.

Hades thought about this and came up with an idea. He would make Meg his prisoner!

Hercules was so upset when he saw Meg in chains that he agreed to a strange bargain. He would surrender his strength for a day if Hades would set Meg free.

"Meg is safe," Hades agreed. "If she gets hurt, you get your strength back."

Hades was ready to put his plan into action. With Hercules out of the way, the evil god would soon rule the world.

First Hades freed the evil Titans from the pit where they had been imprisoned by Zeus. The Titans marched forward, shouting, "Zeus! Destroy him!"

Then Hades ordered the Cyclops, a one-eyed monster, to get rid of Hercules.

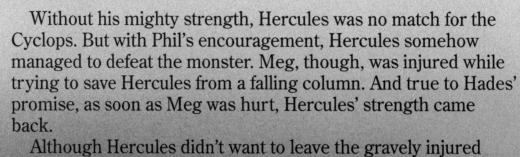

Without his mighty strength, Hercules was no match for the Cyclops. But with Phil's encouragement, Hercules somehow managed to defeat the monster. Meg, though, was injured while trying to save Hercules from a falling column. And true to Hades' promise, as soon as Meg was hurt, Hercules' strength came back.

Although Hercules didn't want to leave the gravely injured Meg, she convinced him to go help his father stop Hades.

Hercules left Meg in Phil's care and hurried to Mount Olympus. He found the gods in chains and Zeus trapped in a mountain of frozen lava. With his bare hands, Hercules ripped open the lava and freed his father. Together they defeated the Titans.

Hades knew his grand plan to take over Olympus was now ruined. As he headed back to the Underworld, he took pleasure in telling Hercules that Meg was dying.

Hercules hurried back to Meg, but her spirit had already left her body. Hercules rushed down to the Underworld, where he saw Meg's spirit floating in a pit of swirling souls.

"Take me in Meg's place!" Hercules told Hades.

That selfless act—Hercules' willingness to give his life for Meg—made him a true hero at last.

On his return to Mount Olympus, Hercules was given a hero's welcome. But he finally knew where he truly belonged—on Earth, with Meg, where together they would live happily ever after.